Ella Plant

Plants a Tree

Written by: Michael S. Amaral

Illustrated by: Shauna Moroney-Hamade

Dedicated to all my family and friends, who have inspired me to pursue my passions, and make this world a better place.

Ella Plant awoke from her slumber to the sound of birds chirping, as she does every morning. Today, Ella arose with added excitement, because she knew she would learn about her new favorite topic in science class at school. As she clamoured about, getting herself ready for school, all Ella could think about were the creatures of the world and their unique habitats.

Ella arrived at school and took her seat in class, paper and pencil set on her desk, ready to learn everything she could. The teacher, Mrs. Raffe, asked for the class's attention and began to teach her lesson. Mrs. Raffe talked about the snow leopards in the peaks of the Himalayas, the bison of the Great Plains, and the whales in the depths of the oceans.

With every new detail that Mrs. Raffe spoke of, Ella continued to fill her paper with notes and asked about other new and exciting species.

After teaching the class about many different animals and their habitats, Mrs. Raffe explained the one thing that threatened everyone, even themselves, and that was Climate Change.

Ella didn't understand and asked Mrs. Raffe, "What is Climate Change and how does it affect everyone at once?"

Before Mrs. Raffe could answer, Leon spoke up and exclaimed, "My dad said there is no such thing as Climate Change!"

Hye, Leon's best friend, started laughing uncontrollably.

Mrs. Raffe turned to Leon and the rest of the class and said gently, "I can assure you Climate Change is a real thing. Just because you can't see it, doesn't mean it is not affecting you or anyone else."

Ella listened intently as Mrs. Raffe explained, "The planet is beginning to slowly warm up, melting ice at the north and south poles. The melting ice is affecting the polar bears in the northern hemisphere and shrinking islands because of rising sea levels in the southern hemisphere."

As class ended, Ella began to feel sad thinking about the planet and all the animals she loved who were in danger. Ella went to her next class, but could not think about history when she now knew there was so much that needed to be done for the future of the planet.

After class ended, Ella asked her history teacher, "Mr. Gutan, what do you think can be done about Climate Change?"

Mr. Gutan thought for a moment, then began to describe the actions that had been taken in the past. Ella listened to everything Mr. Gutan had to say, but all she heard was a history lesson and not what she could do to help.

Ella thanked Mr. Gutan for the information and went to her next class.

Next, Ella went to art class. During art class she wanted to draw a picture of how to protect the planet from Climate Change. Ella asked her art teacher, Ms. Lovebird, how she should draw this. Ms. Lovebird began to describe the most beautiful scene with all of the animals from all around the world.

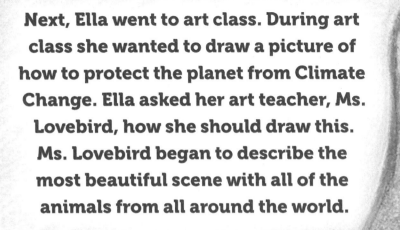

Ella admired the image her teacher described for her to paint, but she didn't just want to draw a picture of a perfect world. Ella wanted to draw a picture of how she could help fix the world she lives in to make it better for everyone. The class ended, and Ella never got to start her drawing because she spent all her time thinking about what to do.

Ella's next class was gym. Gym wasn't her favorite class, but she thought to herself that maybe some exercise could help stimulate some ideas. Ella joined her classmates for a game of Dodgeball, but she couldn't think of any new ideas.

The gym teacher, Mr. Eetta, could tell something was wrong, so he asked, "Ella, is everything okay?"

Ella could not help but to ask, "Mr. Eetta, what do you think about Climate Change?"

Mr. Eetta did not know what to say, so he was honest and replied, "Ella, I do not know much about that subject, but any time I do not know what to do, I like to go for a run."

Mr. Eetta's response did not help Ella at all, but she thanked him and went back to playing the game.

It was the last class of the day and that meant Ella had one last teacher to ask about Climate Change. Ella sat through the entire English class, patiently waiting to ask her teacher, Mrs. Potamus, if she had any answers to her questions.

Mrs. Potamus, admitted to Ella, "I am not an expert on Climate Change, but I do know some books you can read."

Ella wrote down the titles of the books Mrs. Potamus recommended and ran directly to the library.

Ella, ran into the library nearly knocking over the bookshelves. The librarian was known by everyone as Aunty Lope at school. Aunty Lope, scared by Ella's entrance, asked, "Ella, what is your hurry?"

Ella excited and panting from her run replied, "I need to find these books!" Aunty Lope looked up the books and pointed Ella in the direction of where to find them.

Ella sat in the library and didn't leave until she read the two books. After she finished, Ella looked up and sighed, because she still did not have the answer she was looking for. Ella returned the books to Aunty Lope, thanked her, then left to go home. Ella slowly walked home wondering how, after asking all her teachers and reading books, she was not any closer to finding her answers.

As she returned home from school, Ella entered the house visibly upset.

Momma Plant immediately asked, "Ella, what is wrong?"

Ella just replied, "Nothing" to her mother. She thought that if none of her teachers could help her, then her mother would not be able to either.

Her mother tried again, "I know something is wrong. What is it?"

Ella then told her mother what was bothering her.

Momma Plant replied, "Sit down here with me, and I will try to answer your question the best I can." Ella sat with her mother as she explained, "Climate Change is a big issue and not everyone understands what they can do to help, but it is good that you are thinking about what you can do. You may not be able to stop Climate Change from happening, but you can make small changes in your life that can help inspire others to make changes around you."

Ella thought about that for a second and asked, "But what can I do here that can help?"

Momma Plant turned to Ella and asked, "What is something that produces oxygen for everyone to breathe?"

Ella looked at her mother, unsure, and asked, "Trees?"

Her mother looked at her and replied, "Yes. If you do something as small and simple as plant a tree, you are helping make a change."

Ella's excitement grew, "I will tell my friends, and we can do it together!"

The next day at school, Ella assembled her classmates and asked them all if they would plant a tree with her. Every one of them said yes, and they agreed that they should plant the tree at their school. Ella and her classmates immediately went to the principal and asked, "Mrs. Ceros, can we plant a tree here at school to do our part against Climate Change?"

Mrs. Ceros thought about it briefly and replied, "That is an excellent idea, and I will help you plant the tree in the front of the school. Also, I think we should plant the tree on Earth Day, which is April 22nd."

Ella and her classmates all liked that idea and agreed to plant the tree on Earth Day.

Earth Day came, and a group of Ella's family and friends were all there to plant her tree. It made Ella so happy to do something to help with the problem of Climate Change, and it made her even more happy to have everyone she cared about with her. Ella lit up with pride as everyone pitched in to plant the tree.

When Ella returned home she turned to her mother and said, "I'm happy we planted a tree today, but what else can I do to help with Climate Change?"

Momma Plant replied, "Today was a big success. What can you do to bring awareness to more people?"

Ella thought long and hard about how she could do that. After several minutes, the idea came to her like a bolt of lightning. Ella jumped up and exclaimed, "I know! I'm going to host an Earth Day Fair next year!" Beaming with excitement, Ella ran off to start planning her next big project.